STO

jE
Blatch
Going with the flow.

Going with the Flow

Going with the FLOW

by **Claire H. Blatchford**

with illustrations by **Janice Lee Porter**

a first person book

Carolrhoda Books, Inc./Minneapolis

Carolrhoda Books, Inc., c/o The Lerner Publishing Group
241 First Avenue North, Minneapolis, MN 55401 U.S.A.

Website address: www.lernerbooks.com

LIBRARY OF CONGRESS CATALOGING-IN-PUBLICATION

Blatchford, Claire H.
    Going with the flow / Claire H. Blatchford : with illustrations by Janice Lee Porter.
        p. cm. — (A first person book)
    Summary: When Mark changes schools in mid-year, he is angry, lonely, and
embarrassed by his deafness, but he soon begins to adjust. Includes information about
deafness and illustrations of signs.
    ISBN 1–57505–069–2
    [1. Deaf—Fiction. 2. Physically handicapped—Fiction. 3. Schools—Fiction. 4. Sign
language.] I. Porter, Janice Lee, ill. II. Title. III. Series.
PZ7.B6139Go 1998
[Fic]—dc21
                                                                        97-10011

Manufactured in the United States of America
1 2 3 4 5 6 – JR – 03 02 01 00 99 98

This book is a salute to the courage of deaf children everywhere.— C. H. B.

For Ade— J. L. P.

All the kids were staring at me. All twenty-two of them. I could feel their eyes going over my Nikes, my jeans, my T-shirt, my crew cut, my behind-the-ear hearing aids. It was like I was an alien that had fallen out of the sky and landed in New Jersey.

My face burned. I hate it when people stare at me.

I looked at Mrs. Willcox, the fifth grade teacher. I caught a couple of the words on her lips, ". . . can't hear . . . speak slowly . . . "

Then she pointed, first at me and then at the door. A woman had entered the classroom. It was my interpreter, Mrs. LaVoie. Why did she have to come on my first day? Nobody would want to talk to me with a grown-up following me around.

"Hi, Mark. How are you?" Mrs. LaVoie
signed and mouthed the words silently to me
across the room.

The whole fifth grade was watching us.

"This is dumb!" I signed back.

"They've never met a deaf kid before," she
replied. "They . . . "

I didn't wait for her to finish. I had to get out
of there. I raced down the center aisle, nearly
tripped over the leg of some big, long-haired guy
with a smirk on his face, and ran out the door.

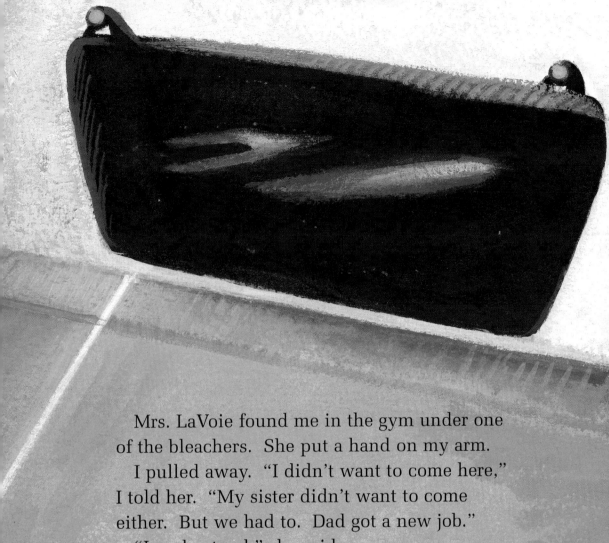

Mrs. LaVoie found me in the gym under one of the bleachers. She put a hand on my arm.

I pulled away. "I didn't want to come here," I told her. "My sister didn't want to come either. But we had to. Dad got a new job."

"I understand," she said.

How could she understand? She didn't know what I'd left behind in Vermont — the mountains, the ski team, Jamie . . .

By now, Mrs. Willcox and the principal were there too. Mrs. LaVoie touched my arm again.

"I'll help you," she promised.

I didn't move. I wasn't going back to that classroom.

I saw the worry in Mom's eyes when I got off the school bus. I knew from her face that Mrs. LaVoie had called and told her I'd spent the day alone in the gym. You don't have to have ears to hear things like that.

Sarah, home early from school, was in the kitchen. Her rusty red ponytail whipped the air as she turned to face me. "I heard all about it! They say I have a freak of a brother."

"The teacher made me stand in front of the class. They were staring at me."

Sarah rolled her eyes. "You think you're the only one? They stared at me too. What do you expect when you change schools in October?"

"But I'm deaf!" I said.

"Deaf!" Sarah shook her head as she made the sign. "So deaf you won't listen to anyone — not even the interpreter they got for you?"

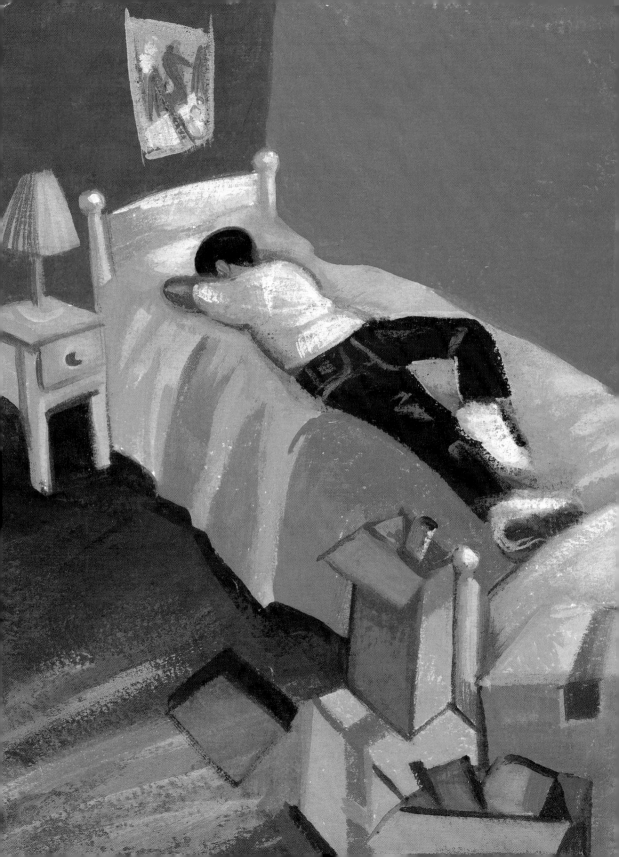

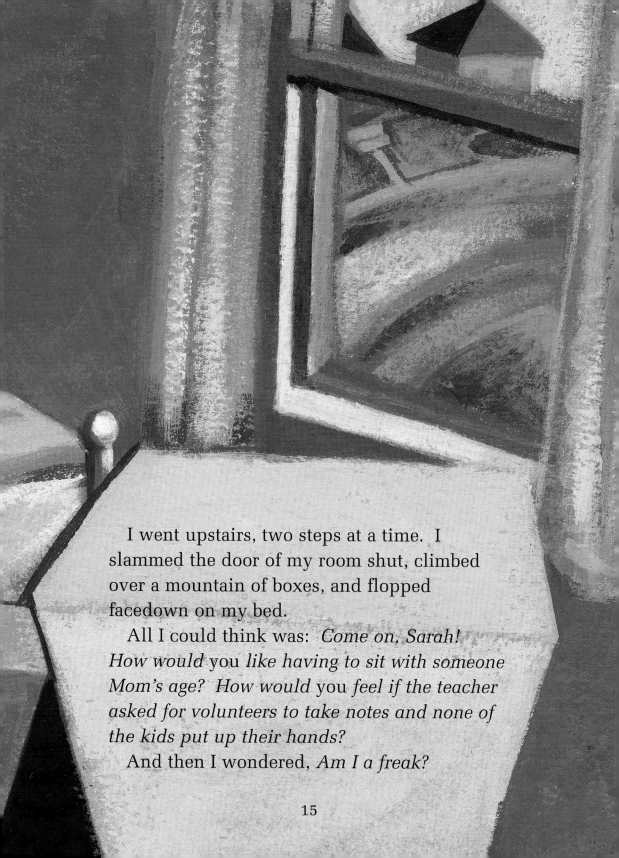

I went upstairs, two steps at a time. I slammed the door of my room shut, climbed over a mountain of boxes, and flopped facedown on my bed.

All I could think was: *Come on, Sarah! How would you like having to sit with someone Mom's age? How would you feel if the teacher asked for volunteers to take notes and none of the kids put up their hands?*

And then I wondered, *Am I a freak?*

15

I fell asleep. Being deaf is tiring. You have to look, watch, listen, and figure out what's going on all day long. It was like this in Vermont too. But at least there were other deaf kids, kids that knew signs.

Dad's hand woke me, pressing down on my shoulder. I almost didn't open my eyes. I was sure he was mad.

"Supper time," he said. His blue eyes seemed far away behind his thick-rimmed glasses.

I nodded.

"I heard about today," he said.

I shrugged.

"When you make a change, the first few days are always the hardest."

I didn't say anything.

"Did you hear me?" Dad asked.

The words popped out before I could stop them. "Dad, can I go back to Vermont? Maybe I could live with Jamie."

Dad's eyebrows went up. They do that when he doesn't know what to say. He doesn't really know Jamie's parents. They're deaf and they only sign.

"If you did that you'd never talk," Dad said.

"Signing *is* talking."

"I know, but . . . " His eyebrows rose again. "So . . . you're comfortable with Jamie's family?" he asked.

I paused to think about it. Jamie's parents don't think I'm really deaf. I wasn't born deaf, the way they were. I had meningitis when I was three, and everyone in my family but me can hear.

All I knew then was that I wanted to be skiing with Jamie when the snow came. I'm faster than him, but he's sharper on the corners. Real sharp. But there I was in the middle of flat, brown, dull New Jersey.

Dad waved to get my attention. "I tell you what, Mark," he said. "I'll think about it. But you have to promise to try one week of school here."

I put a hand over my mouth to hide my grin. *One week? That's nothing.*

It was cold and gray the next morning. I
wondered if it was snowing up north. I'd tried
calling Jamie three times on my TDD — that's a
telephone device for the deaf — but no one
answered. Where was he? Had he forgotten
about me already?

At school the big guy I'd nearly tripped over
was sitting on my desk. My stomach tightened.
What was going on?

When he saw me coming, he hopped down.
"I'm . . . eeeth," he said.

Eeeth? "Teeth?" I asked.

He nearly fell over laughing. The other kids
laughed too.

Mrs. LaVoie tapped at my arm. "He's telling you his name." She spelled it out with her fingers. "K-E-I-T-H."

My face started burning again. Keith, not teeth. Some words look alike on the lips. Why had I opened my big mouth?

Keith held up a notebook and a pencil. "I'm . . . taking . . . notes . . . for . . . you," he said.

I wanted to sink through the floor and out of sight. I hate it when people mouth everything and talk like I'm two years old. Everyone was watching us.

Only one week of this, I thought grimly as I reached for the chair to my desk.

Mrs. LaVoie's lips and signs were easy to read. At noon she said she was going home for lunch and would be back after recess.

Keith dropped a couple of tightly folded pages on my desk and ran out.

The only free seat I could find in the cafeteria was near some third graders. I read a book so I didn't have to look at them while I ate. I wasn't very hungry.

When I stepped outside at recess, I saw a bunch of guys playing basketball. They were really into it. Their tongues were almost hanging out of their mouths.

I wanted to watch them, but I didn't want them seeing me. I turned to go and ***whack!*** Something hit me hard on the neck. There was Keith, his long hair plastered to his sweaty head. I knew from the way he was grinning that he'd thrown the basketball on purpose.

"Come play," he gestured.

I glared at him. He'd called me just like you'd call a dog. I would have gone back inside except for the look on his face. I could hear it as clearly as I hear the thoughts in my own head: *What a wimp! Is he going to run away and hide again?*

I put the book and my lunch box down and walked onto the court.

"You're . . . on . . . *my* . . . team," Keith said, using preschool language again.

"You don't need to talk so slow," I told him.

"Oh —" The way Keith said it I realized he wasn't sure I could really talk.

One of the guys tossed the ball to me. I caught it and ran off dribbling.

They were fast, but I was faster.

I ran this way and that. Around them, between them, maybe even under them. Anger can give you speed.

I took a wild shot, missed the basket, dove for the ball, got it, and dropped it.

Someone tripped me up from behind. I went flying, hands first, onto the pavement.

It was Keith.

"You — *you* did that?" I yelled.

He waved his fist at me. "Who do you think you are?" he yelled back. He was talking fast now. "*I'm* the captain. You do what I tell you."

We stared at each other. I could have quit, but I didn't want to. It's weird, but I *had* to find a way to stay on that team. I *had* to show him I could do it the way he wanted.

I got up. The palms of my hands were stinging, but I didn't look at them. "What do I do?" I asked.

Keith paused and scratched his arm. "Watch," he replied.

Watch? That's what I do all the time.

"Flow," he added. "Yeah, go with the flow."

I didn't try to call Jamie that night. I was
too busy thinking about Keith and basketball.
When I skied, it was my speed against Jamie's
speed. This was different. I'd never really
played *with* other guys on a team before.
Would Keith ask me to play again?

For the next three days straight, I played
basketball with Keith at recess. Sometimes I
could see the others shouting and laughing. I
couldn't understand them and felt really out of
it. Sometimes Keith and the others shoved me
around. Once when that happened I got angry.
Keith had tripped me again. I was ready to
punch him. But when I saw the look on his face,
I suddenly knew he wasn't trying to make me
mad. He was just trying to tell me how to flow.

Friday, after the last bell, Keith dropped his notes on my desk.

"Thanks, but I don't think I need them," I said.

He frowned. "How come? Aren't they good enough for you?" he asked. He was angry. It was like I'd tripped *him*. Neither of us said anything then because Mrs. Willcox was coming toward us wondering what was going on. We didn't want her in on the conversation.

"I'm not sure I'm coming back," I told him when we were outside. "That's why I said that about the notes."

His mouth fell open. "But you just got here," he said.

I told him about Jamie and the school in Vermont.

"You can't go . . . . " Keith was talking a mile a minute now, jumbling the words, gesturing wildly. I had to make him say it over.

He told me that tryouts for the basketball
team were coming up soon. "You've gotta try
out," Keith said, grabbing my arm. "You're fast,
you're smart, and you don't need ears like
everybody else to hear what's going on.

"Besides," Keith went on, "if you made the
team, we could use sign language."

My bus pulled up then. I had to go. When I
looked out the window, Keith put two fingers
up in a big *V*. I read the words on his lips, "We
need you."

We need you. No one had ever said that to
me before. It felt good.

Well, that was two months ago, and I'm still in New Jersey. And, yes, I'm on the basketball team. I'm teaching the guys some sign language. It comes in handy when we're playing other schools!

Keith still trips me up every now and then when I get going all by myself on the court. He still takes notes for me too. (Some of his notes are really about basketball, but don't tell!)

I'm not saying everything is fine. When you're deaf, you're always deaf. You can't get over it the way you get over a broken leg or a headache. People forget to look at you when they talk. Or they forget to slow down a little or not mouth everything. Or they have trouble understanding what you're saying.

I know there will always be times when I feel left out. But that's okay. I'm learning to go with the flow.

Author's Note

Some people, like Mark, lose their hearing because of illness, sudden injury, or because of genetic factors. Others are born deaf. Each person's experience of deafness is different.

It is usually difficult for those who are born deaf to learn to speak, because they have no sense of the sounds of words and of how loud their voices are. It is hard to imitate sounds you can't hear. Those who lose their hearing later may continue to use speech and may need therapy to help them feel, rather than hear, the words they speak.

Mark wears behind-the-ear hearing aids and is quite self-conscious about that. Why? Because they show the world he is deaf. And some people are either afraid to talk to a deaf person or they are put off

This sign means "pass." Move your right hand forward, past your left hand, with your palms facing each other and with your knuckles facing out.

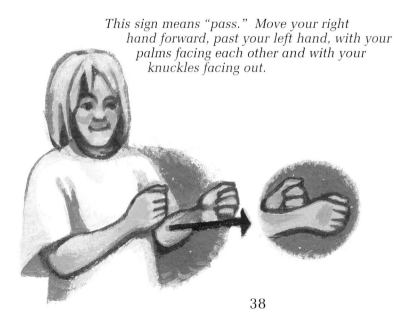

when a person with a hearing aid has difficulty understanding them.

Hearing aids do *not* automatically enable a person to hear. For one thing, the ability to recognize specific sounds may have been damaged. Also, the ability to block out distracting noises in order to hear certain things — you may do this when listening to your mother while the radio is on — may have been damaged. Mark's hearing aids help him to know where sounds are coming from. They also help him determine how loud sounds are.

Most deaf people use their eyes, not their hearing aids, to "hear." They read signs, lips, facial expressions, gestures, and body movements. Whether you are deaf or you can hear, be sure to look *at* a deaf person when you speak. Let the person know what you are talking about.

This sign means "run." With both of your index fingers pointing out and your palms facing each other, repeatedly crook both index fingers and your right thumb while moving your hands forward.

You may also want to learn some sign language. Not all deaf people use sign language, and there are variations among those who do use it. Both American Sign Language, known as ASL, and signed English use finger spelling (the hand forms letters of the alphabet to spell out words) and signs (one sign may stand for a whole word or common phrase). Some common signs from ASL — what Mark taught his teammates — appear on the preceding pages.

Although each person's experience of deafness is different, the common need among all deaf people is the need to communicate. For language — whether spoken, signed, or written — connects us, makes us truly human, and helps us to go with the flow of life.